# MOUSE'S

Lauren Thompson

ILLUSTRATED BY Buket Erdogan

SIMON & SCHUSTER BOOKS FOR YOUNG READERS

New York London Toronto Sydney

To Dan and Anna—L. T.

To all of the children of the world
who are our sunshine and inspiration,
and to my sunshine, Yagmur—B. E.

SIMON & SCHUSTER BOOKS FOR YOUNG READERS
An imprint of Simon & Schuster Children's Publishing Division
1230 Avenue of the Americas, New York, New York 10020

Book design by Mark Siegel
Manufactured in China
10 9 8 7 6 5 4 3 2 1
CIP data for this book is available from the Library of Congress
ISBN 0-689-85835-3

first edition

One sunny
summer day . . .

Mouse and Minka came
along to play!

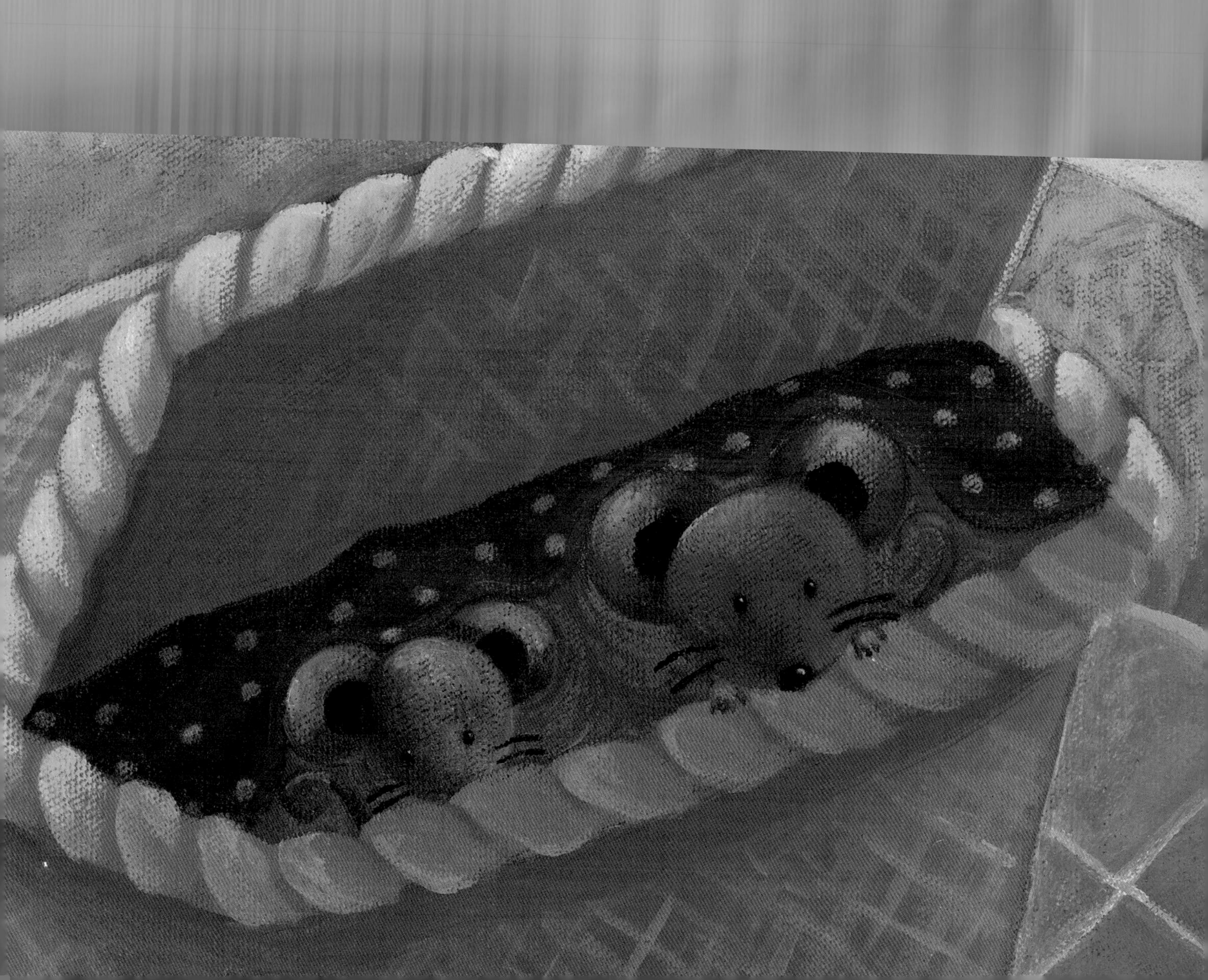

Tiptoe quick,
off went Minka.

"Wait for me!"
said Mouse.

*What's over here?*
wondered Mouse.

Drippy, sweet,

wet, red

watermelon.

"Tasty!" said Minka.

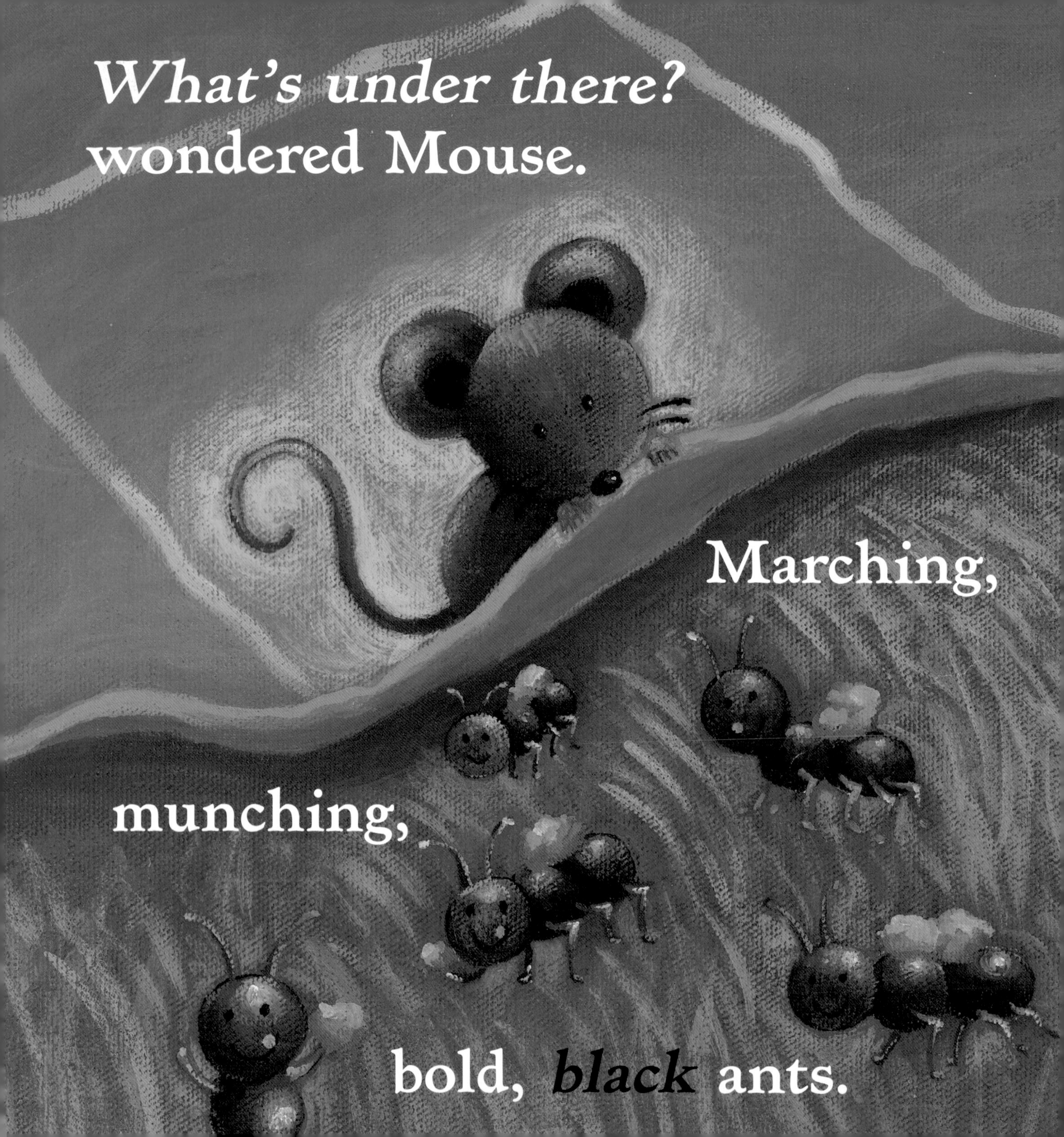
*What's under there?*
wondered Mouse.
Marching,
munching,
bold, *black* ants.

"Out of the way!" said Minka.

*What's down there?*
wondered Mouse.

Tipsy-tumbly,

tickly,

green grass.

"Whee!"
said Minka.

What's up there?
wondered Mouse.

Oh, so high,

bright

blue sky.

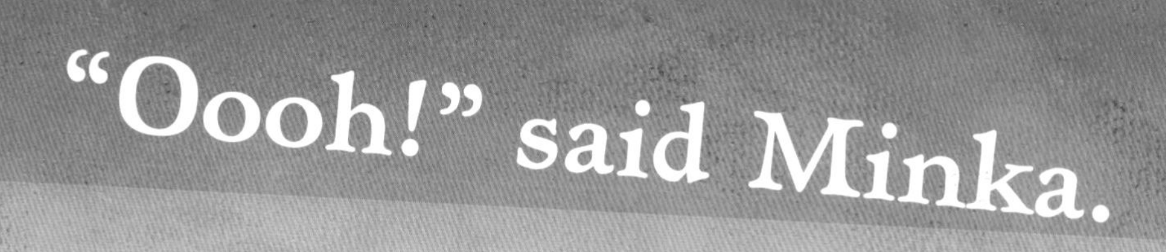

“Oooh!” said Minka.

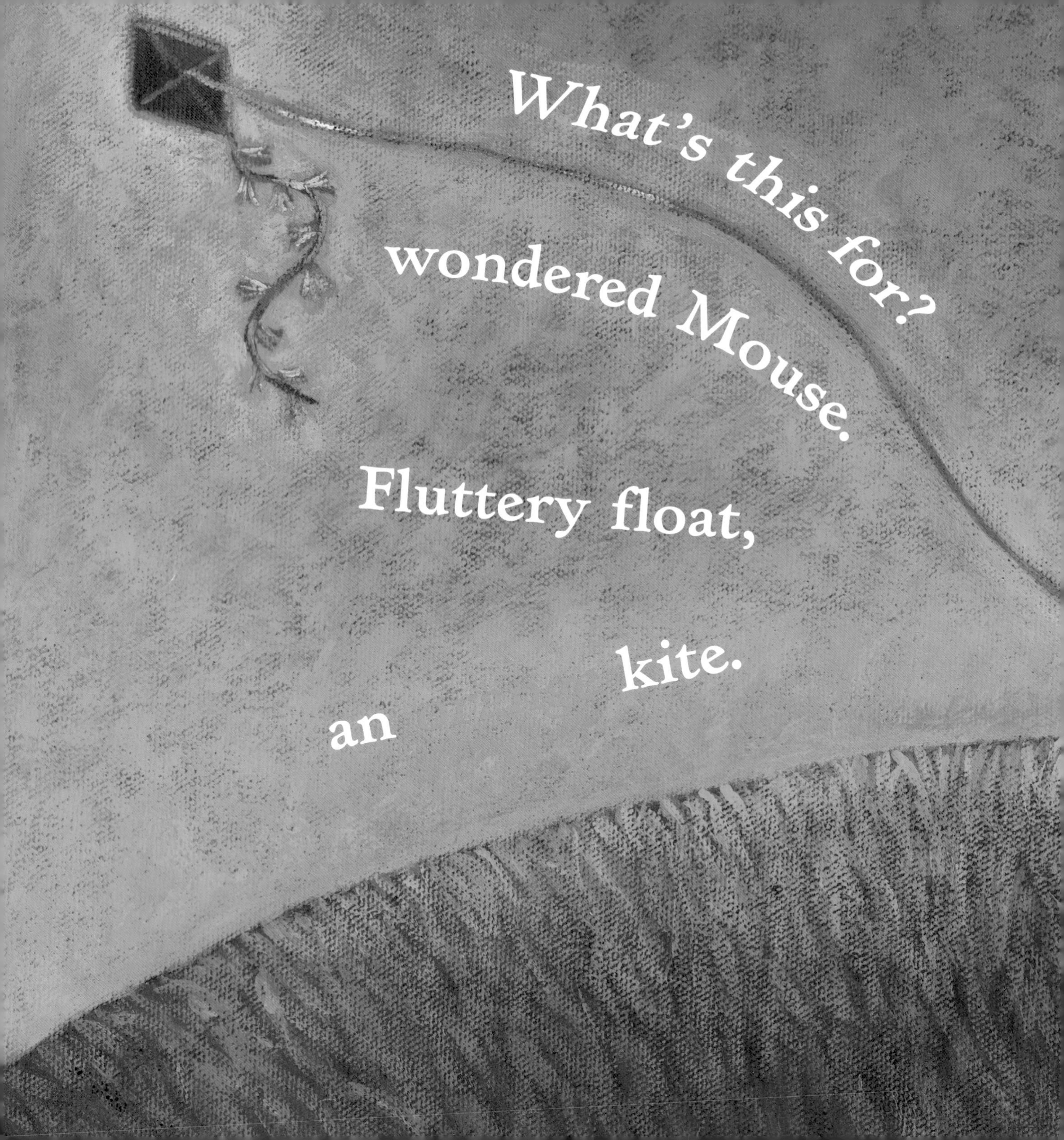

What's this for?
wondered Mouse.

Fluttery float,

an kite.

"Hold on!" said Minka.

*What's in here?*
wondered Mouse.
Sweet-tart sip,
yellow
lemonade.

“Ooops!” said Minka.

What do we
do with this?
wondered
Mouse.

Nibbly crumb,
soft
white
bread . . .

and sticky, smooth,

brown peanut butter . . .

and jiggly drip,

*purple* jelly.

"YUM!" said Minka.

*Oh! What's all around?*
wondered Mouse.

Wink, blink,

fireflies glowing.

“Try to catch one!”
said Minka.

Then
*CRACKLE!*
*POP!*
*BOOM!*
*What's THAT?*
wondered Mouse.
Fireworks fly,
*every color* in
the sky.

“Hooray!” said Minka.

"Hooray for summer,
Mouse!"